Tomorrow is the First Day of School

Maureen MacDowell • Illustrated by Max Hergenrother

Wading River Books
PO Box 955
Wading River, NY 11792
www.wrbooks.com

Institutional discounts available for bulk sales. Please contact us at buydirect@wrbooks.com

Printed in the U.S.A
1st Edition

The illustrations in this book were done using watercolor, pencil and mixed-media
Text type used is Futura – a letter accurate font for children.

ISBN: 978-0-9791463-0-5

Library of Congress Cataloging-in-Publication Data

MacDowell, Maureen.
 Tomorrow is the first day of school / written by Maureen MacDowell ; illustrated by Max Hergenrother.
   p. cm.
 Summary: A little girl is nervous about her first day of school, but when she gets there she discovers that it is someone else's first day of kindergarten too.
  ISBN 978-0-9791463-0-5
 [1. First day of school--Fiction. 2. Kindergarten--Fiction.] I.
Hergenrother, Max, ill. II. Title.
  PZ7.M15845To 2007
  [E]--dc22
                                        2007014184

"The child-soul is an ever-bubbling fountain in the world of humanity"
Friedrich Froebel, the founder of Kindergarten

For Mom and Dad, I love you – M.M

For the women who made this possible, my wife and mother – M.H

A special thanks to Ross – M.M and M.H.

Tomorrow is the first day of school.
I'm very nervous going to school for the first time.
Will all of the children be friendly?
How about all of the teachers – will they be friendly too?
What is it really going to be like?

Mom keeps telling me that everything will be great.
She even made me my favorite dinner to help me feel better.

Mmmmmmm...
mashed potatoes with gravy and meatloaf!

I am picking out my clothes before I go to bed. I am packing my backpack, too. I don't want to forget anything on the first day of school!

It's getting late. I really should go to sleep.

Mom and dad kiss me good night and tell me to have sweet dreams.
Easy for them to say, they don't start school tomorrow!

I know we will do lots of different things.
We are going to color, paint, read storybooks and count.

I've already met some of the children in my class.
I just know we're going to have a lot of fun!

Oh, I am still so nervous. I can't sleep.
What if the children don't like me?
What if the other teachers don't like me?
What if I forget all my work at home?

I can feel the butterflies flying around inside my tummy
and it isn't even morning yet.
Will I ever be able to sleep?
What if I can never sleep again?

Zzzzzzzzzzzz.

"Wake up honey. Today is the big day.
The first day of school is here and you don't want to be late," said mom.

"Okay, I guess I better get up, but I think I might be coming down with something. Maybe I can start tomorrow instead?"

"Your breakfast is on the table, now get ready for school."

I bet everyone will really like my dress a lot.

My backpack is brand new, my lunch is packed, and mom made my favorite breakfast...

...chocolate chip pancakes with ice cream and whipped cream! Wow, this really is turning out to be a great day!

I see the bus coming down the block,
so that means it's time for me to go to school.

"Make sure you kiss your father good-bye," mom said.

I'm acting really brave,
but I still feel those butterflies in my tummy.
Here I go, off to school. I know I can do it.
I am going to have a great day!

There's the school.
Maybe I'll just wait outside.

Well, everyone else is going in.
I guess I better go in now.

There's my classroom. It looks so nice.

There are lots of books and tables and toys and children.
Oh, I hope they like me.

"Good morning children, I'm going to be your kindergarten teacher. My name is Miss Barbera and today is my first day of school, too!"